The Hit and Run
GANG 8

PRIDE OF THE ROCKETS

Don't Miss Any of the
On-the-Field Excitement with
THE HIT AND RUN GANG
by Steven Kroll
from Avon Books

(#1) NEW KID IN TOWN
(#2) PLAYING FAVORITES
(#3) THE SLUMP
(#4) THE STREAK
(#5) PITCHING TROUBLE
(#6) YOU'RE OUT!
(#7) SECOND CHANCE

STEVEN KROLL grew up in New York City, where he was a pretty good first baseman and #3 hitter on baseball teams in Riverside Park. He graduated from Harvard University, spent almost seven years as an editor in book publishing, and then became a full-time writer. He is the author of more than fifty books for young people. He lives in New York City and roots for the Mets.

The Hit and Run GANG 8

PRIDE OF THE ROCKETS

STEVEN KROLL

Illustrated by Meredith Johnson

AN AVON CAMELOT BOOK

THE HIT AND RUN GANG 8: PRIDE OF THE ROCKETS is an original publication of Avon Books. This work has never before appeared in book form.

AVON BOOKS
A division of
The Hearst Corporation
1350 Avenue of the Americas
New York, New York 10019

Text copyright © 1994 by Steven Kroll
Illustrations copyright © 1994 by Avon Books
Illustrations by Meredith Johnson
Published by arrangement with the author
Library of Congress Catalog Card Number: 93-91019
ISBN: 0-380-77369-4
RL: 2.8

First Avon Camelot Printing: July 1994

CAMELOT TRADEMARK REG. U.S. PAT. OFF. AND IN OTHER COUNTRIES, MARCA REGIS-TRADA, HECHO EN U.S.A.

Printed in the U.S.A.

OPM   10   9   8   7   6   5   4   3   2   1

For Elvin Montgomery

Contents

1. A Bad Mood   1
2. Doing the Unthinkable   8
3. Grand Slam   14
4. Consequences   22
5. Misery   30
6. Mr. Old Reliable   39
7. Dancing   45
8. Release Time   51
9. New Tricks   57
10. Trying's Part of the Fun   63

1. A Bad Mood

It was a chilly Tuesday afternoon. Dressed in their sweats, the Raymondtown Rockets were finishing up fielding practice at the ballfield down behind the IGA.

The whole team was out of sorts, and not just because it was cold and the baseball stung when anyone caught it. Having won a real squeaker, 2–1, last Saturday against the Bradford Wildcats, they'd come out on Sunday and blown a game 3–2 to the Bombers in Healesville. The worst thing about the loss had been the three errors committed by Rocket infielders in the bottom of the sixth. The errors had brought in two runs and cost the team the victory.

Big, blond Justin Carr, the Rockets' dominating

first baseman and sometime pitcher, was in an especially lousy mood. Though he didn't make many errors, his misplay had been the first in that embarrassing sixth inning. With nobody out, he had bobbled a bunt that allowed the runner on first to get to second and the hitter, who had planned a sacrifice, to reach first safely. Those two runners had been the ones who came around to score.

It didn't matter to Justin that he had pitched well against the Wildcats on Saturday and had not only won the game from the mound but also had the game-winning hit. It didn't matter that after his error, Phil Hubbard had lost a fly ball in the shadows behind third and Brian Krause had booted a ball at short. Without his mistake, there would have been one out and only one man on. The whole outcome of the game could have changed.

Coach Jack Carr, Justin's father, was fungoing the ball to the infielders. Coach Herman Lopez was doing the same in the outfield, and Justin stole a moment to watch as his twin sister, Jenny, the Rockets' left fielder, shagged a fly ball from between two other outfielders.

2

The moment lasted too long. Coach Carr caught him looking and cracked a sharp ground ball in his direction. Playing at the edge of the outfield grass, Justin recovered quickly. He got down, speared the ball on the big hop, and waited a couple of seconds as Andy McClellan, the Rockets' pitching ace, hurried over and covered first. Then he tossed the ball to Andy at the bag for the out.

"Good going!" Coach Carr shouted, then fungoed a shot to Brian at short. Brian cross-stepped to his right, backhanded the ball, whirled, and fired low to first. Justin was waiting, both heels touching the base. Now he went into his stretch, right foot touching first at an angle and the left leg extended with the knee bent. The ball smacked into his trapper's mitt. He pegged it home to Luke Emory, the Rockets' hustling catcher.

"Nice play!" Coach Carr yelled. He stepped in front of the plate. "Okay, that's it for fielding. We'll start batting practice now, but pitchers will go to the bullpen for some work with Coach Lopez first. Everyone has to be sharp against the Rams tomorrow."

Andy, Justin, Brian, and Josh Rubin, the little sidearm fastballer, got their gear and headed for the bullpen. On the way, Justin saw Jenny trekking in from the outfield. He waved, and she waved back.

When the four pitchers arrived at the pen, Coach Lopez was waiting. As they slumped side by side on the rickety bench, the coach said, "Hope you're ready for a workout. Andy's up first. He's starting tomorrow."

Tall, dark Andy removed his Rockets' jacket, wiped the shock of hair out of his eyes, and walked to the mound. Coach Lopez grabbed the bullpen catcher's mitt and crouched behind the plate.

Andy threw a few fastballs, moved them up and down, mixed in the occasional change-up. The change-up was missing the corners.

"You're aiming it too much," Coach Lopez said. "Loosen up. Get the ball in the back of your palm, and just let it go."

Andy listened, went back into his windup, and tried again.

"Well done," said Coach Lopez. "You caught the outside corner. Keep it up."

5

Andy did, throwing more change-ups, then going back to the fastball, then mixing up the two, looking more and more accurate as he ticked off his thirty pitches.

Justin didn't mind having to wait. After all, Andy *was* the starting pitcher in tomorrow's game and number one in the rotation. Justin watched the way he raised his hands winding up, the way he controlled his leg kick and the pace of the ball. He could always learn something from Andy.

First baseman, pitcher, Justin also batted cleanup. Though he would never say, he was proud of those positions. He was also proud that he was the player the coaches could rely on, especially in the clutch. Never mind that error from the other day. How many times had he dug the ball out of the dirt and saved a run? How many times had he stepped into the batter's box with the game on the line and delivered the big hit that had won it for the Rockets?

And when it came to pitching, Justin was second only to Andy and in many ways the steadier of the two. When a starter faltered, he could almost always be counted on to step in and cool the opposition bats. And when he started, he was consistent, threw low strikes, and got the batters out. He was also one of the few lefties in the league who wasn't a little wild.

Because of all these things, he expected to be called second.

Andy stepped from the mound and retrieved his jacket.

"Good outing!" Coach Lopez shouted. "Okay, Brian, you're next."

2. Doing the Unthinkable

Never a complainer, never one to get annoyed, Justin's mouth dropped open as red-haired Brian took Andy's place.

Behind his thick glasses, Brian was a pretty good pitcher. He was reliable, he threw strikes, and occasionally his fastball had pop. But he was hardly ever overpowering, and he was hardly ever asked to start a game. Mostly he was the team's surehanded regular shortstop. When he was brought in to pitch, it was usually for spot relief.

But here he was, following Andy on the mound in practice. He threw a few pitches, and Coach Lopez jumped up. "You're overthrowing. Take a deep breath. Relax."

Brian did, and he got better. Never terrific, Justin noted silently, but better. As Brian's pitch count wound down, Justin got ready.

"Okay, Josh," said Coach Lopez. "Let's see what you can do."

By now, Justin was seething. He'd been left for last, and it wasn't right!

Josh began throwing some of his crazy sidearm fastballs. He could be effective, but he could also be very erratic.

"You're not seeing the plate," Coach Lopez called. "You're way outside on everything."

They worked on that for a while. Then Josh finished up with some eye-popping sidearm smoke.

"Nice work!" Coach Lopez shouted.

Josh grinned and gave the coach a thumbs up sign. Then he bopped off the mound and returned to his seat.

"Okay, Justin."

The coach sounded tired, as if Justin were some kind of afterthought. Justin couldn't believe it. He strolled to the hill, squeezed the ball hard, wound and threw a change-up. Then he walked around a little, stepped to the rubber again, and threw a fastball.

Coach Lopez stood up. "You're pointing your left shoulder too much toward first."

Justin nodded. Smoothing out his anger, settling in, he turned his shoulder more toward the plate on the next two pitches, both of them fastballs. He could feel the difference, knew the ball was coming in low.

"Excellent!" Coach Lopez said after the second pitch. Then he hurried toward the mound.

"But I asked you to throw last today for a reason. There are a few other things we need to work on."

Justin frowned. He stood on the rubber, fingering the baseball. He couldn't think of anything else he might be doing wrong.

"The problem," Coach Lopez continued, "is the slowness of your delivery, the way you walk around on the mound and take so much time between pitches. Runners have been stealing on you, and we . . ."

Justin was no longer listening. He was willing to learn from anyone, but Coach Lopez wanted him to change his whole style of pitching! That didn't seem right. He was the one they could rely on. So what if a few runners stole bases? He usually picked them off anyway.

Justin dropped the ball and walked off the mound.

"Where are you going?" Coach Lopez asked. "We have work to do!"

Justin turned. "With all due respect, sir, I think my pitching has been important to this team. I don't think I should have to make these changes."

Avoiding the shocked looks of his teammates, he kept walking, gathered up his gear, and left the bullpen. He crossed the outfield grass and sneaked behind the home team dugout, hoping no one would notice him. Then he hurried to the station wagon in the parking lot.

It wasn't locked, and he scrunched down in the front seat. He would miss batting practice as well as the rest of his time on the mound. It wasn't okay, but he would have to live with it.

He could hear the shouts as Luke drilled one, obviously very deep. Then Jenny came up and clearly did the same. That satisfying click of bat against ball kept sounding in his head, but it couldn't matter now. His pitching style had saved

lots of games for the Rockets. He'd never been so insulted in his life!

Justin kneaded the pocket of his pitcher's glove, that glove, so perfectly fitted to his hand. He looked at his fingers. He looked at the dashboard. He looked out at the other cars in the parking lot.

Gradually his anger fell away. It began to sink in what he had done. Members of a team *always* listened to their coaches. Going against that rule, for whatever reason, was unthinkable.

He began to realize he was embarrassed by how he'd behaved. Justin Carr, team leader, acting like a rookie! But he was also worried. What would happen now? Would he be punished? Would he be thrown off the team?

He didn't know, and he had no idea what he could do to make things right.

3. Grand Slam

Justin could hear practice breaking up, the Rockets leaving the field and gathering their gear. "Good luck tomorrow!" Phil Hubbard shouted to Andy.

Voices and footsteps came closer. Justin scrunched down further in his seat so he wouldn't be seen.

Suddenly the driver's side door opened. His father, big and broad, stood looking in at him.

Justin felt like a little kid caught doing something wrong. His father kept looking at him, his lips tight together, his hands on his hips, until Justin sat up straight and looked back. Then Coach Carr stepped inside, slid behind the wheel, and slammed the door.

14

He stared through the windshield. "Coach Lopez told me what happened. I figured I'd better let you cool down and not disrupt the rest of practice. Jenny's over by the dugout. I asked her to wait so we could talk."

Justin knew he should say something. No words came out.

Coach Carr continued. The sentences came in bursts. "The coaches are here to help. You know that. You're one of the best players on the team. What kind of an example do you think you're setting? You're also my son!"

The last barb hurt the most. But Justin was too overwhelmed to admit his father was right, that it had all been a terrible mistake, and he was embarrassed by it. He couldn't explain how he'd been in such a bad mood anyway and how he, the most reliable Rocket, had been insulted and . . .

"I didn't want to do what he said," Justin replied.

It was the wrong thing to say, totally wrong, but there it was, said.

Coach Carr bristled. "That's an unacceptable answer, Justin, and certainly unacceptable coming

15

from a ballplayer as good as you. I'd better get Jenny."

He was back in a moment. Jenny followed, looking hesitant. Tentatively, she climbed into the backseat.

Coach Carr yanked open the front door, sat behind the wheel, and slammed the door a second time.

Apart from the starting of the engine, there was no other sound all the way to Broadview Avenue. Up Market Street, past the elegant shops on Symington Boulevard, it felt as if everyone were choking. Occasionally Justin's angry, frightened eyes found Jenny's in the rearview mirror. He couldn't tell what she was thinking.

At home Justin went straight to his room. He sat on the bed, feeling bruised and helpless and wanting to fight back. He looked around—at the Rockets pennant on the wall, the trophy for best athlete in second grade. Then he went to the closet and pulled out his uniform.

Good old number 7. Mickey Mantle's number! He was proud to wear it. Would he ever get to wear it again?

16

"Justin!"

He put the uniform back in the closet and went to the door. "Yes, Mom."

"Dinner's ready. Would you please come now?"

"I don't feel like dinner. Could I skip it tonight?"

Mom looked concerned. "It's chicken a la king, your favorite."

"I just don't want any."

There was a pause, then, "Well, okay, but if you want to talk, I'll be around later."

"Thanks, Mom," Justin said, but he knew he didn't want to talk. He wanted to be left alone so he could figure out what to do.

Nothing came to him, but later on, when dinner was over, he got hungry. He tiptoed to the kitchen, took the leftover chicken a-la-king out of the fridge, and put some on a plate, with a few green beans to go with it. He heated everything up in the microwave, poured himself a glass of milk, and carried it all out onto the big front porch. His parents were in the living room watching TV, but they didn't notice him go by.

He sat on the soft sofa with the busy flower print, eating and watching the sky darken and the moon rise. He heard the screen door slam and wondered who it was. It was Jenny.

She sat beside him, pulling at her ponytail. "Hi," she said.

"Hi," said Justin. "What are you doing here?"

"I came to look at the stars. What do you think I'm doing here? I'm worried about you."

"Well, I'm glad you're worried too. I'll probably be kicked off the team."

"It would never happen. Coach Channing thinks too much of you. Besides, Dad wouldn't let it happen."

"He might not have a choice."

"Justin, why didn't you listen to Coach Lopez? Why did you make such a scene?"

"I don't know. I was insulted. Now I'm embarrassed and mad. I don't know what to do."

He tried to keep his lower lip from trembling. He tried to keep from bursting into tears.

"You're never like this," Jenny said. "The only time I can remember you going off the rails so completely was when I made those terrible er-

rors and lost you that game against the Tornadoes. You were so mean to me!''

''We made things up, though.''

''Of course, but do you remember what you said when we did? You said I was a *ballplayer,* that every ballplayer makes mistakes and has to bounce back from them. Well, you're a ballplayer, and you have to bounce back!''

Justin laughed. ''I hope I get the chance.''

''There's something else, too. Nobody's perfect, Justin. Even though you're awfully good, you'll always have stuff to work on, just like the rest of us.''

Jenny got up and hugged him. Then she went back inside.

Justin knew Jenny was right. He was glad she had been brave enough to speak her mind. But he still didn't know how to solve his problem. At this point, he didn't even know how big his problem would be!

He stayed on the porch a long time, wrestling with his hurt, thinking about what Jenny had said and how to bounce back from his mistakes. He listened to the crickets chirping and the occasional shadowy car passing by at the end of the drive-way. Then he got up, closed the screen door qui-etly, and returned to his room to try to finish his homework.

4. Consequences

When the alarm rang the next morning, he couldn't get himself out of bed. His first thought was, how could he face his father? The next was, how could he face his teammates at school?

He was still lying there, covers pulled up to his chin, when his mom banged on the door. "Justin, you'll be late!"

For a second he thought about pretending to be sick. He knew it wouldn't work. "Okay, Mom, coming!"

He rolled out of bed and into some clothes, washed up, brushed his teeth, and made it to the kitchen in time to gulp a glass of orange juice and grab a bagel he could eat in the car. He kissed his mom good-bye.

"Are you all right?" she asked.

Coach Channing always asked that when a pitcher messed up and he had to make a trip to the mound. Justin smiled. "Sure, Mom, I'll work it out."

Then he was out the door and down the front steps.

The station wagon was waiting in the driveway. Justin was relieved to see Jenny already sitting in the front seat. He slipped silently into the back, and his father turned the key.

It was a pretty spring morning. They pulled out onto Broadview Avenue and then into heavier traffic. As Jenny and Justin compared notes about the arithmetic problems from last night, Jack Carr concentrated on one block of slowly moving vehicles after another.

Finally turning into the school driveway and coasting to a stop before the glass front doors, he coughed once and faced his children.

"I have to meet with a client this afternoon, so I can't be at the game. I'm sorry about it, but Mr. Wong will drive you."

Coach Carr was a lawyer in Raymondtown. He

frequently had to miss mid-week games. This was nothing new.

"It's okay, Dad," Justin said.

"We'll *try* to do without you," Jenny added.

But Coach Carr wasn't finished. "Of course, Justin, you realize there will be some consequences from yesterday."

Jenny glanced back at Justin. His face was ashen.

There was a silence. Then Jenny and Justin kissed their dad on the cheek, tumbled out of the car, and dashed into school. As usual, their baseball gloves were sticking out of their backpacks.

Knowing that everyone on the team would be aware of what had happened yesterday, Justin wondered if anyone would say anything. As he and Jenny burst into Mrs. Irvington's classroom, he noticed Luke whisper something to Andy. Andy nodded, leaned over, and said something to third baseman Phil Hubbard.

Well, that wasn't so bad. Justin sat down in his seat in the second row. Jenny went to hers in the third. As they got comfortable, Pete Wyshansky, the world's most loudmouthed right fielder, bellowed, "Look, there's Justin Carr! No one's better than Justin. He doesn't even have to listen to the coaches!"

Justin wanted to hide inside his desk. He wanted to sink into the floor and disappear. But he had his pride. He just sat in his seat, looking straight ahead and blushing, his hands folded in front of him.

"All right, Pete," Mrs. Irvington said, "that's enough of that. Baseball matters should be settled at the baseball field. I hope we can begin the day now."

All through the morning, through language arts, math, and social studies, Justin sat quietly in class. Pete's words echoed in his head, but so did his father's. What were the "consequences from yesterday" going to be?

Fortunately Mrs. Irvington seemed to understand his unhappiness. Probably responding to Pete's remarks, she seemed to draw an imaginary ring around Justin and leave him alone. All morning long, he didn't have to answer a single question.

Now he had to get through lunch. He hoped he

25

would be left alone again, but he was not so lucky. Brian Krause sat right beside him.

At first no one spoke. Then Brian mumbled through his tuna sandwich, "Coach Lopez was pretty mad after you left practice."

When Justin didn't answer, Brian went on. "Jeez, Justin, why didn't you go along with him? Who knows what will happen now?"

Justin's anger flared, but he said nothing. At least the rest of the team didn't know what the consequences were going to be before he did.

He choked down the rest of his sandwich and a little dish of canned pears. As he was getting ready to leave, Pete appeared from nowhere.

"Everyone bow!" he yelled, bowing himself and gesturing. "King Justin is leaving the room! Everyone bow to the king!"

Justin wanted to shout back at Pete and shake him, but of course he couldn't. He was so humiliated, he could hardly get through the afternoon. By the time he and Jenny piled into the backseat of Mr. Wong's green Saab, he was hoping for a few moments of nothing but peace and quiet.

There weren't. Mr. Wong, who usually said al-

most nothing, asked if they were excited about the game.

Justin's heart sank as Jenny and Michael Wong, the Rockets' center fielder, began chatting about the team and how they'd beaten the Rams at home the last time and how they hoped to do it again away. But fortunately this conversation carried them all the way across town to the Rams' field. Justin got to look out the window and worry. He didn't have to say a single word.

"Good luck," Mr. Wong said as the three Rockets clambered out of the car. Trying to be nice, trying to avoid his fears, Justin said, "Thank you, sir."

Even though it was a mid-week game, the parking lot seemed full of cars. As Jenny, Michael, and Justin ran toward the field, the bleachers already held a number of people, mostly Ram fans, of course, in green and gold caps.

Out in the field, the Rams were already practicing. Their green and gold uniforms gleamed in the sun. Next to the Rockets' red and white, they looked like peacocks.

The rest of the Rockets trickled in and slapped

hands. As Coach Lopez led them in windsprints and stretches along the sidelines, they got a view of the starting pitcher they would have to face.

He was a huge blond kid with long lank hair. Make him a little shorter, cut his hair, and he'd have looked a lot like Justin. He had a wicked fastball, a deceptive change-up, and the kind of strength that was sure to mean stamina. His name was Dave Nordstrom.

When the Rockets dashed onto the field for their fifteen-minute pre-game practice, Coach Channing called Justin back. Paralyzed, rooted to the spot, Justin somehow managed to trot over to his coach.

"I want you to go out and practice with the rest of the team," Coach Channing said, "but I'm benching you for today's game. You'll have to apologize to Coach Lopez before you start again."

5. Misery

Justin felt as if a bucket of cold water had been dumped over his head. He'd never been benched before, never missed a starting assignment. He steadied himself, knowing he had to run back onto the field. At least he hadn't been dropped from the team!

Hours seemed to have passed, but when Justin appeared in the infield, no one even realized he'd been gone.

But Justin knew, and as he went about catching pop flies, then moving over to take his turn at first base, there was a strange fluttering in his stomach, a feeling that for the first time he didn't belong. Once he'd practiced a few minutes and loosened up, he felt more like himself again.

He scooped a couple of throws out of the dirt, grabbed a grounder down the line, ran over and caught a tough pop foul near the stands, came up to bat and belted two good shots to right.

He was ready to play, but of course he wouldn't. As he returned to the dugout with the rest of the team, he felt as if he'd survived his own death notices, only to discover he was dead after all.

He found a place on the bench as Coach Channing posted the starting lineup. He watched from a distance as the members of the team trooped up to read it.

''What's this?'' he heard Luke yell. ''Justin's not in the lineup. Hey, guys, look!''

Coach Channing took Luke aside. There was some heavy, garbled discussion. Justin heard Luke say, ''I know he shouldn't have done it, but how can you make the whole team suffer? We need him out there. You know that.''

There was a pause, and Coach Channing said, ''I understand, Luke, but there are some things that cannot be tolerated.''

And that was that. Luke turned away and col-

lapsed beside Justin on the bench. He put his arm around him.

"I'm sorry, kid, but you really seem to have blown it. We'll have to win today without you."

Looking at the ground, Justin nodded.

"Okay!" Luke said, and slapped hands. "You'll just have to root extra hard for us so we can do our jobs. Are you ready for that?"

Justin managed a small smile. Luke was trying so hard to make him feel better. "Yeah, I'm ready."

"Good," Luke said, and stood with the rest of the team for "The Star-Spangled Banner."

As Dave Nordstrom finished his warmup pitches and Luke, leadoff hitter extraordinary, was taking some practice swings in the on-deck circle, Justin sneaked over and checked the lineup. Ken Bernstein was starting at first base and batting sixth. Brian would bat cleanup, with Pete fifth. All right, let's see what they could do without him!

Justin wished he really meant that. Of course he wanted the Rockets to win. He just hated being on the bench so much. As the game began, he sat, miserable and fuming, hardly able to pay attention.

Fortunately Luke's spirit seemed to infect his teammates and things began well for the Rockets in the top of the first. Luke himself popped up to third leading off, but Phil singled up the middle and Andy doubled him home with a shot to the gap in left-center. Dave Nordstrom, man mountain in green and gold, seemed hittable after all.

With Brian coming up, Nordstrom seemed ready to try nothing but heat. He got one by on the outside corner, but then he hurled two balls. Adjusting to his new role in the cleanup spot, Brian worked the count to 3 and 2, then singled through the hole between short and third. Andy came sliding home, beating the throw to the plate by at least two feet.

Pete struck out and Ken Bernstein grounded into a force at second, but the Rockets took the field leading 2–0. And Andy came out smoking in the bottom of the first. He struck out leadoff man and left fielder Champ Mayfield, then came back and struck out third baseman, Penny Woo, and got Nordstrom, batting in the third spot, to fly to left.

Maybe he was mad at getting jammed by the

pitch he flied out on, but Nordstrom, facing the bottom of the Rocket batting order, was a different pitcher in the bottom of the second. His fastball had pop and sizzle, he threw an across the seamer that was unhittable, and his change-up had the hitters reaching and missing. Jenny bounced to the mound, Michael popped to second, and Vicky Lopez, getting better wood than the others, lined out to short.

Meanwhile, Justin was still on the bench, getting more and more unhappy. He wanted to be out there helping the team, and when the next Ram batter, cleanup man and right fielder Ricardo Suarez, slashed a grounder to Phil at third, he held his breath. Phil misplayed the ball off the heel of his glove and had to hurry his throw. Ken Bernstein couldn't scoop the ball out of the dirt, it got by him, and Suarez ended up at second.

If I'd been out there, Justin grumbled to himself, I'd have caught that ball.

Now things began to come apart. With a count of 2 and 2, center fielder Leroy Jennings doubled to the right field corner, sending Suarez home. Frustrated by this, still haunted by Phil's and Ken

Bernstein's errors, Andy served up a first-pitch meatball to the catcher, Bobby Martinelli. Martinelli crushed it over the left field fence, and the Rams led 3–2.

By this time Justin was dying. He pounded the pocket of his glove and shouted ''Let's go, Rockets!'' but it all felt terribly futile. There was nothing he could do that would make a difference.

Luke and Coach Channing went out to the mound to talk to Andy, and that seemed to settle him down. He got out of the inning with a grounder to second, a grounder to short, and a pop foul Phil leaned into the bleachers to catch at third. Justin was relieved to see Ken Bernstein handle the throws to first on both grounders without a hitch.

In the third, both pitchers seemed to take command. Luke lined a single to left leading off, then stole second on a wild pitch to Phil. But that was it for the Rocket action, and Andy got three quick outs in the bottom of the inning.

Pete singled to center to open the fourth, but Ken Bernstein bounced into a double play. After Jenny walked and Michael squibbed a checked-swing single to right, Vicky popped up to the catcher.

In the bottom of the inning, Andy was still strong. He punched out Ricardo Suarez with fastballs, then lost Leroy Jennings on a close pitch on the outside corner. With Jennings on first, Andy tried to pick him off, but Ken Bernstein, obviously nervous, missed the ball. Jennings went to second.

Flustered, definitely upset, Andy toed the rubber and walked Bobby Martinelli on four pitches. Vicky and Brian went over to talk. Andy nodded, nodded again, and ground the ball into his glove. Then he threw two fastballs by first baseman Ted Schwartz and on the very next pitch caught him lunging at a change-up. Schwartz hit an easy fly to Jenny in short left, and no runners advanced.

But Andy wasn't out of the woods yet. Shortstop Phyllis Brown looped a single to right, and Jennings came around to score on a throw from Pete that missed the cutoff man and caromed off the backstop.

If Ken Bernstein hadn't screwed up, Justin thought, Jennings might have been picked off! Maybe he wouldn't have scored!

37

That was all for the Rams, but the Rockets came up in the top of the fifth trailing 4–2.

Quickly Luke singled down the third base line, Phil struck out swinging, Andy walked, and Brian beat out an infield hit off the glove of shortstop Brown. The bases were loaded for Pete Wyshansky.

Pete muscled his way to the plate. Nordstrom reared back and hurled a fastball. Pete was taking all the way, but the pitch was on the inside corner for Strike 1. Two balls followed, but then Pete got his pitch, a fastball down and in. He swung mightily and hit a towering pop-up to third base. He was automatically out because of the infield fly rule.

Two outs now and Ken Bernstein coming up. But wait. Bernstein was being called back.

"You're still benched, Justin," Coach Channing growled, "but I can't make the whole team pay. You're going to pinch-hit."

6. Mr. Old Reliable

Justin blinked in disbelief. He got to his feet and stretched. Then he smiled, went to get his bat, and stepped into the on-deck circle for a few practice swings with the doughnut.

Even though he hadn't played in the game, his swing felt good. He walked to the plate, knowing he could do something.

If Nordstrom had been throwing junk, Justin would have stood far forward in the batter's box. Because he had such a mean fastball, Justin stood way back. He anchored his rear foot and checked Coach Lopez at third for the sign.

Coach Lopez touched his cap. Two outs, bases loaded, hit away. Justin was pretty sure that's what it would be, but these coaches were gamblers. You could never rule out a suicide squeeze.

Justin dug in, got his arms up and back, and faced Nordstrom. Lefty against rightie, power against power. The crowd grew quiet and intense.

Pitching from the stretch, Nordstrom hurled a fastball. Justin wasn't swinging; he wanted to see how Nordstrom threw before he committed himself. The fastball was on the outside corner.

"Strike 1!" the umpire yelled.

Justin stepped out and knocked some dirt out of his sneakers with the end of his bat. He checked the sign again. Still hit away.

He stepped back in, but this time, when the fastball came, he tried a fake bunt. He pulled his bat back in time, but the Ram infield, drawn in for a play at the plate, went scrambling.

It took them a moment to recover as the umpire called Ball 1, but Nordstrom was unflappable. Never mind the fake bunt or the lousy pitch. He came back with yet another fastball, a real sizzler that caught too much of the plate.

It was the pitch Justin had been waiting for. He snapped his wrists, and the ball took off. Going,

going—the crowd gasped as it began to look like a grand slam.

The ball carried far but not far enough. It bounced off the right field wall, and when Suarez couldn't get to it, Justin slid into third with a three-run triple. With one swing of the bat, he had put the Rockets ahead 5–4.

"Rah Rah Rockets!" came from the small crowd of visiting Rocket fans. *"Rah Rah Rockets!"*

Clearly Dave Nordstrom was shaken. His coach came out to talk to him, along with first baseman Schwartz and shortstop Brown. He stayed in the game but promptly gave up a clean single to left to Jenny. To a smattering of high fives, Justin trotted home with the sixth Rocket run.

That was all for Nordstrom. In came a scrawny lefty with no stuff at all but lots of control. Ed Beard struck out Michael Wong on four pitches, and that was it for the Rockets.

But the damage had been done, and as the team took the field, Justin heard, "Jordan Smithers, take over at first."

Justin exchanged a look with Coach Channing. He adjusted his cap and stayed on the bench.

42

Andy was tiring but somehow slithered through the bottom of the fifth. Jordan Smithers helped by fielding a crucial bunt and firing to second to keep a Ram runner from reaching scoring position. But when the Rockets did nothing against Beard in the top of the sixth, Brian came in to finish the job.

Suarez flied deep to center with one gone, but that was the most the Rams could muster. As the final out smacked into Jordan's mitt, Justin cheered and the Rocket fans went wild.

The team trotted off the field. When Luke and Jenny reached the dugout, they highfived Justin. The Rockets had a 6–4 victory, and coming off the bench in the clutch, he had been their main man.

Yeah, Justin thought to himself. They can insult me, bench me, think I don't listen, but I'm still Mr. Old Reliable. Even so, he felt a little off balance. Hot and sweaty but still fresh, the glow of his achievement surrounded him. At the same time, he couldn't help realizing that of all the Rockets, only Luke and Jenny had just highfived him. Would there be any end to this business with Coach Lopez? He wished it had never happened or could somehow be wiped away.

Starting home in the station wagon, sitting in the front with Jenny in the back, he heard his father say, "You did well this afternoon, Justin. No sulking when you got benched, and when you got back into it, you made the difference."

"Thanks, Dad," Justin said, hoping that would be all.

"But you'll still have to apologize to Coach Lopez," Dad added. "You treated him quite badly, and he does have things to tell you that you should learn."

So there was the bottom line. He'd proved again he could be counted on, but that wasn't enough. He'd been rude to Coach Lopez, and he had to apologize. He still wasn't sure he could do that, but he had to do something. He had to get back in the lineup. Mr. Old Reliable couldn't do the team any good on the bench.

7. Dancing

When they reached the house, Dad immediately told Mom about Justin's clutch performance. Given the conversation in the car, Justin was surprised.

But it certainly was nice when Mom said "Justin, you're terrific! Congratulations."

With that happy beginning, dinner and the rest of the evening became quite lively. There was lots more talk about the game, everyone had seconds on everything, and Jenny and Justin spent a half hour discussing and laughing about the stories they had to write for language arts.

All this made for a good distraction, but it didn't help Justin figure out what he was going to do. When he got to school the next morning, he hoped everyone would be so excited about yesterday's win that he could keep feeling good about that at least. Walking in the door with Jenny, he pretended to get ready for the congratulations, the highfives.

Nothing happened. Andy passed by in the hall and said "Good job, Justin," and Pete had the good grace to ignore him, but everyone else sort of ignored him too.

At lunch he groused to Jenny about nobody appreciating what he had done.

"They're team players," Jenny said. "You know what that means."

Usually a team player himself, Justin felt stung—and angry all over again. "But I was just defending myself! Don't I have the right to do that?"

Jenny shrugged and shook her head.

After lunch, there was music, and at music there was suddenly dance class. It was the second time Mrs. Johnson, the music teacher, had organized this, and she was obviously pleased. With a big smile she announced, "We're going to practice the fox-trot again. I hope you all remember what we did the other day."

Justin and Vicky had been partners the first time around and had done really badly, so badly that when Vicky stepped on Justin's foot and he yelled "Owww!" she ran out of the room. But in last Saturday's game against the Wildcats, Vicky had helped Justin out of a pitching jam with an unassisted double play. She'd also begun the crucial sixth inning rally that had won it for the Rockets.

After the game, Justin had promised Vicky another shot at dance class. He'd hoped it wouldn't come around for a while, but there it was, just a few days later.

As the rest of the class milled around choosing partners, Justin walked right up to Vicky. "Want to give it a try?"

Vicky smiled. "So you didn't forget."

"Nope."

"Let's go then."

They got into position as Mrs. Johnson trilled several times on the piano. "All right, class, remember, you are practicing the box step. One-two-three-four. One-two-three-four."

She began to play. The different couples shuffled around the floor. Just like last time, Andy McClellan and Andrea Pfister looked the best.

But Justin and Vicky were trying very hard. Slowly they moved around, sometimes even watching their feet. "One-two-three-four," Justin said, guiding Vicky. "One-two-three-four. One-two-three-four."

Vicky seemed to be having trouble moving backwards, something that was never a problem when she played second base. She didn't seem to like having Justin lead. But he was patient with her, as patient as he could be. Gradually they began to resemble partners.

The first time Vicky stepped on Justin's foot, they stopped and looked at each other. Justin started laughing. Vicky laughed, too, and they were over the hump.

Now it didn't matter if anyone's foot got stepped on. It was just part of the whole experience, and they began moving faster, Justin still helping Vicky but Vicky catching on and beginning to glide. Not only were they moving faster, they were moving farther, too! Soon they had covered most of the room, while many of their classmates were still stuck in place.

At the end, Mrs. Johnson came over and put

her arms around them. "You looked great today. You haven't been practicing in secret, have you?"

"No, Mrs. Johnson," said Vicky.

"Too much baseball for that," said Justin.

From the look on Vicky's face, Justin could tell how pleased she was. For reasons he could not explain, he was happy, too. As the two of them left the music room, they reached out and slapped hands.

8. Release Time

When the bell rang for dismissal, Justin told Jenny he wasn't going to take the school bus home with her. He wanted to walk over to the ballfield and do some thinking. He'd get a lift back or take the bus up Market Street and be home before Mom and Dad got there.

Jenny understood. "Okay, Justin. Whatever you want."

It was a bright, sunny afternoon, but that didn't help Justin straighten out his mood or put the pieces together. He walked slowly, weighing one thing against another. When he reached the ballfield, he expected to find it empty. It was not.

Luke was behind the plate. Brian was pitching to him, and Phil was out at second base.

Looking over his shoulder, Luke called, "What's happening, man?"

"I just needed a place to go," Justin said.

"Want to join us? I'm working on my release time down to second. Too many runners are stealing on me."

"But almost no one steals on you," Justin said, except, he thought but didn't say, when I'm doing the pitching. He had to admit, his slow delivery sometimes forced Luke to hurry his throw.

The thought brought him up short as Luke said, "Well, enough of them are."

Justin remembered how back before the season started Luke had asked him and Jenny to come out to help Phil, who'd done so terribly at tryouts he hadn't made the team. "Luke," he finally asked, "is my release time too slow?"

Luke smiled. "I don't pretend to know everything about pitching, but I watch you more than anyone. Yes, my man, I would say it was."

Justin sucked in his breath and made a decision. "Can you help me?"

"Give me a few minutes."

When Luke had made a few more crisp pegs

down to second, he got Justin on the mound. "Okay. First, stop walking around so much. You know that puts the infielders to sleep. Next, I think your leg kick is too high, and when you've got men on, sort of slide your leg toward the plate instead of lifting it if you're not pitching from the stretch. You'll lose some speed on your fastball, but you'll save those stolen bases. Now try."

Justin did a few stretches, then began to throw. He tried the slide step in his motion, and it felt awkward. He kept trying, and it began to feel better. After a while, he seemed able to alternate it every so often with his big windup minus a little height in the leg kick.

"Looking good!" Luke said as he finished.

Justin nodded and moved over to first so Phil and Brian could get in some fielding practice of their own. Afterwards, he thanked Luke. "I really appreciate what you did."

"Don't mention it," Luke replied. "Glad we were here. Just remember, nobody's perfect. We all need a little help from time to time. Want a lift? My dad's coming by."

"That's okay. I think I'll take the bus."

He was pleased by the offer, but he needed some time alone. As the bus rolled up Market Street, he came to some conclusions.

He had liked helping Vicky learn to dance. Luke had liked helping him with his delivery. Jenny and Luke had both said nobody was perfect. Everyone had something that needed improving. Coach Lopez had been right about Justin's pitching style, but even if he hadn't been, Justin should have listened to him. Tomorrow, at practice, he would apologize.

At dinner he told his father what he'd decided. Coach Carr—then Mom and Jenny too—got up from the table and hugged him.

Arriving in the dugout the next afternoon, Justin followed through. Coach Lopez was changing into his sneakers when Justin came up.

"I'm sorry," Justin said. "I was wrong."

Coach Lopez patted him on the shoulder. He seemed grateful that the incident was over.

"Could we try working on your suggestions?" Justin added. "I'd really like to now."

"Of course. Join me in the bullpen when you finish batting practice."

55

Justin took some grounders and pop-ups at first. He took throws from all over the infield and sliced a few shots to right and right-center when it was his turn to bat. Then he hustled over to the bullpen.

Coach Lopez began by saying almost exactly what Luke had said, but he refined it more. "It's not just a matter of the slide step. Sometimes you hold the ball or throw over. Sometimes you quick-pitch to the plate or throw up your front elbow as you come forward. Mix up your moves, and you'll confuse the baserunner and the hitter. With so much going on, there won't be time to steal."

Justin tried everything. The moves still felt a little foreign when they finished, but he liked the possibilities. As they were leaving the bullpen, Coach Lopez said, "By the way, you're starting tomorrow against the Jugglers."

From the bench to the mound in one quick jump! Justin was so astonished, all he could do was grin.

9. New Tricks

When Justin told Jenny, she gave him a big hug. He was so excited, he could hardly get to sleep. He was also nervous. With Josh starting last time out, the Jugglers had walloped the Rockets 8–4 at home.

Coach Carr drove the twins to the game. There was a lightness of feeling in the station wagon that almost made it seem like a new car. When Justin strode to the mound for some practice pitches after stretches, that same feeling was still with him. He had all these new additions to his repertoire. He couldn't help but win.

The Jugglers had a sleek fastballer named Kent Ruffins. He set down the Rockets in order in the top of the first. Then it was Justin's turn.

He struck out the leadoff hitter, then gave up a line drive single to center on a fastball that didn't tail. Vicky leaped, but she had no chance. With one out and a runner on first, Justin tried throwing over, tried holding the ball, tried throwing up his front elbow and delivering a quick pitch to the plate.

The pitch so surprised Luke, he dropped the ball. Butch Eisenberg, the shortstop and runner at first, reached second easily.

Justin got flustered, something he almost never did. Maybe these new tricks weren't for him. Maybe he'd better stay with what he knew. He pounded the ball into his glove and started walking around on the mound the way he used to. On the very next pitch, a change-up low and away, he stepped off the rubber.

''Balk!'' the umpire called.

Eisenberg trotted down to third, and Justin, trying to watch him, trying to regain his concentration and his confidence in Luke and Coach Lopez, uncorked a wild pitch! Eisenberg scored, stamped on the plate coming in, and the Jugglers led 1–0. As if this were not enough, Danny LaMotta, the

third baseman and number three hitter, crushed the next pitch into the left field seats.

Score 2–0, Jugglers.

Luke and Coach Channing came out to the mound. Two runs were just two runs, they said. Relax. Throw strikes.

Justin nodded and tried to get comfortable. From behind, he heard Vicky yell, "Burn it in, Justin!"

"Yeah, burn it in!" shouted Phil.

"Yeah, do it!" said Brian.

Justin took a deep breath and popped up Ruffins. Then he struck out the catcher, Bernie Wiley, and was out of the inning.

But everything got worse in the second. Ruffins was perfect once again, a one-two-three inning. Justin seemed to be back on the mound before he knew it, and he wasn't ready. Struggling to find his rhythm, trying to work fast and keep the hitters off balance, he gave up a base hit, another steal (despite using the slide step), a walk, and a home run.

What was going on? Instead of helping him win, his new approach was helping him lose.

When Coach Channing brought Brian in to pitch and sent Justin over to first, the Jugglers were ahead 5–0.

The Rockets never recovered. Except for a home run by LaMotta in the fourth, Brian kept the Juggler bats in check, but Ruffins' stuff was awesome. Phil and Andy hit back to back doubles in the top of the sixth. That was about it for the Rockets' offense. Final score: Jugglers 6, Rockets 1.

Shoulders hunched, the team gathered their gear in the dugout. Justin sat on the bench. He dropped his first baseman's mitt between his legs and looked at the ground. He'd listened to Luke and Coach Lopez. He'd tried to do what he was supposed to do and messed up. The result: a blowout.

Luke came by and draped an arm around his shoulder. ''Hey, come on, soldier, it happens. They were just real good today. Your new moves'll start working. You'll see.''

Then Coach Channing announced that Josh Rubin would be starting the home game against the Panthers tomorrow.

Justin tried to forget today's loss and turn his

attention to tomorrow. He had to play an outstanding first base, had to make up for his wretched pitching display and his 0–4 performance at the plate this afternoon.

His dad came by, looking to start home. "Ready?" he asked.

"Yeah, I'm ready," Justin replied.

10. Trying's Part of the Fun

Justin and Jenny arrived at the ballfield early. They did their warmups together and played a little catch. Then, just in case, Justin threw a few pitches with Jenny catching. By the time the rest of the team arrived, the two of them were already set to go.

In their black caps with the white panther on the front and their black uniform shirts, the Panthers were as intimidating as ever. But Josh came out meaning business in the top of the first. He threw two sidearm fastballs by shortstop Max Hobart, then got him on a weak ground ball to Vicky. The rest of the Panthers didn't fare much better. By the top of the fifth inning, they had scattered only three hits and hadn't scored a run.

y, facing their former nemesis, An-
gela Faber, the lethal lefty with the jumping fastball, the Rockets had pounded out eight hits and
scored three runs. Justin had a single, a double,
and two RBI's in the effort. He'd also made two
sparkling plays at first to keep runners off the
bases.

But in the top of the fifth, Josh got a little wild.
He hit the third baseman, Larry Jordan, then threw
the ball past Justin at first, trying to pick him
off. Jordan went all the way to third, and when
grandstanding Pete Wyshansky tried for an over-
the-shoulder basket catch and misplayed Cindy
Beranski's towering fly into a double, Jordan
scored.

3–1 Rockets, with nobody out. Josh didn't seem
about ready to get anyone out either. When he
threw a wild pitch to the backstop and Beranski
moved to third, Coach Channing yanked him and
brought in Justin!

Justin really was ready. As he took his warmup
pitches, practicing the big windup, the slide step,
and throwing up his front elbow as he came forward, he knew he had good stuff and good con-

trol. The fastball was sizzling. The change-up was dropping in over the corners just right.

Also, the jitters from yesterday were gone. He remembered the Panther hitters from his last outing against them. He was on the mound, and he would do the job!

The first thing he did was pick Beranski off third. With a 1 and 2 count on center fielder Jeff Klein, she had a three-step lead. Justin's throw was so unexpected, she hardly moved. All Phil had to do was charge down the line and tag her.

This so unnerved Klein that he struck out flailing on the next pitch, a fastball at the knees. With two outs and one to go, gruff Max Hobart was coming up again.

Hitless in three trips to the plate today, Hobart was always a threat. A contact hitter, he could pull the ball with power. For that reason, he usually stepped in the hole toward third when he swung.

Justin thought he had Hobart's number. When a batter stepped in the hole, he brought his bat with him. Pitch him outside, and he'd never reach the ball.

So Justin fired low and away, then high and away, then low and away again. The first two pitches were strikes, the third was a ball. Then Hobart started fouling everything off.

Knowing that the more pitches he threw, the more likely Hobart was to connect, Justin remained cool. Slowly, ever so slowly, the count went to 3 and 2.

Justin summoned up his best effort. Using the high—but not quite as high—leg kick with no one on base, hoping the batter would be confused and commit too early, he fired a fastball down and away.

Caught off balance, Hobart swung. No one was more surprised than he when a little nubbler trickled back to the mound.

Justin picked up the ball and fired a strike to Josh at first. The crowd cheered *"Rah Rah Rockets!"* They were out of the inning and still ahead, 3–1.

The Rockets could get nothing going in the bottom of the fifth. Angela Faber was just too tough. But Justin came out to pitch the sixth feeling confident. He'd done it last inning. He would do it again. Three more batters. Three more outs.

But with the count 1 and 1, Freddie Berman, the mean little second baseman, slashed a single to right. With nobody out and the tying run coming to the plate, would the Panthers try to move the runner?

Chuck Reese, the big first baseman, dug in. He had a long stride, lowering both his body and his bat. Justin knew he'd never get the bat back up in time to hit the high pitch.

As Justin decided how to pitch to Reese, he was also aware of Berman at first. He threw over to keep him close. Then he went to the slide step for a strike on the outside corner.

Luke lobbed the ball back to him, and Justin threw over once more. Berman danced back to the bag. He knew he couldn't take too many chances.

Justin went to the slide step again and missed the outside corner for a ball. If he was going to get beat, it would have to be high and inside or high and away.

With the ball back in his glove, he checked Berman at first. Then he held the ball for a moment, quick-pitched from the stretch, and the runner was going! Justin could almost see Luke smile as he rifled the throw to Vicky at second. Berman was out by at least a step.

The brashness of the play and the accuracy of the throw seemed to deflate the Panthers. With the count 2 and 2, Chuck Reese lofted a soft fly ball to Michael Wong in center. Then skinny Ben Lord, heavyhitting cleanup man, worked the count to 3 and 1 and popped up to Brian at short.

The game was over. The Rockets had the win 3–1.

As the crowd went wild and the players began running off the field, Luke and Justin walked toward each other. Halfway between the mound and home plate, they highfived and shook hands.

''Well,'' said Luke, ''practice makes perfect.''

''No,'' said Justin, ''nobody's perfect, but trying's part of the fun.''